To Gabrielle
–CL

For my two little mice
–AE

This edition produced 2004 for
BOOKS ARE FUN LTD
1680 Hwy 1 North, Fairfield, Iowa, IA 52556 by
LITTLE TIGER PRESS
An imprint of Magi Publications
1 The Coda Centre, 189 Munster Road,
London SW6 6AW, UK
www.littletigerpress.com
First published in Great Britain 2004
Printed in China
1 3 5 7 9 10 8 6 4 2

JUST FOR YOU!

by Christine Leeson

Illustrated by Andy Ellis

LITTLE TIGER PRESS

Jenny opened her eyes. It was a sweet summer morning and it was so early the sun was barely up.

"Wake up," Jenny whispered to her brothers and sister. "It's Mom's birthday today. We have to wrap her present."

All the mice jumped out of bed.

"I'll help!" cried Jenny's sister excitedly.

"I'll help, too!"

"And, me!"

Jenny stepped back as the mice
pushed forward. "Be careful!" she
cried. "You'll break...!"

SMASH!

It was too late. The present
was pulled from Jenny's paws
and shattered on the ground.

"Oh no," said Jenny, looking
at the broken gift. "Maybe we can
find something else before Mom
wakes up. Come on, everybody!"

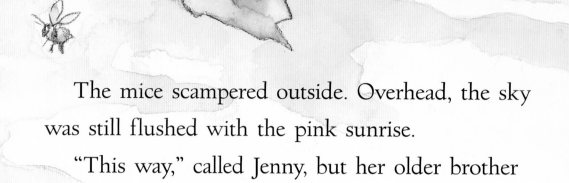

The mice scampered outside. Overhead, the sky was still flushed with the pink sunrise.

"This way," called Jenny, but her older brother had already seen something in the shadows.

"Look, look!" he shouted. "How about these?"
Next to the path there was a cluster of juicy red
strawberries.

"Mm, what a treat!" Jenny said, licking
her lips. "Mom will love them!"

At that moment Vole scurried out of the dewy grass.

"Thank you," she said. "You've found my strawberries. I was carrying some home for my family's breakfast when I dropped a few. I've really got my paws full here!"

"Oh," said Jenny, feeling disappointed. "We thought we'd found a present for our mother."

"Maybe she'd like something else instead," said Vole. "How about those?" She nodded toward some feathers caught between two branches of a nearby bush.

"Oh yes! They'll make a lovely soft pillow!" said Jenny, and she scampered off to gather them. "Mom will be so surprised. This is going to be the best birthday present ever!"

But just then Bluejay chirped from above,
"My feathers! Thank goodness you've found
them. I need them to line my nest and keep
my eggs warm."

"You'd better take them then," said Jenny.
"They would have made a nice present for
our mother's birthday, though."

Bluejay thought for a moment. "Does your mother like flowers?" she asked. "I can see a nice one in the grass just over there."

"Oh thank you!" cried Jenny, and the mice scurried off as fast as they could.

The grass was very tall and the little
mice had to push and scramble through it
in search of the flower.

"I can't see it anywhere," cried Jenny.

"I see it!" shouted her little brother.
"Quick, Jenny! Over here!"

He picked up a large white daisy and waved it over his head. "Do you think Mom will like it?" he asked, stumbling under the flower's weight.

"She'll love it!" Jenny said. "It will make a beautiful present! Let's hurry back home before she wakes up."

Just then Rabbit hopped over. "Wait,
wait!" he called. "That's my flower! My
grandma's not feeling well and I was going
to take it home for her. I put it down for
a minute and then it was gone."

"Oh, we're sorry," said Jenny. "You should take it for her. We can find another present for our mother."

"Thank you, little mice," said Rabbit as he hopped away. "I hope you find something soon."

Jenny scratched her head. The sun was
climbing over the trees into the deep blue sky.
Their mother would be waking up soon and they
still hadn't found a birthday present.

Suddenly something fluttered across the path.
Jenny leaped up and grabbed it...

but it was only a piece of paper, not nearly pretty enough for a present.

"We'll never find anything! Mom's birthday will be ruined!" Jenny burst out. The mice began to cry. Big tears plopped down onto the back of the paper.

"Stop," sniffed Jenny. "We're making it all sticky."

Then she suddenly had an idea. "Wait here!" Jenny squeaked. "I'll be back in a minute."

Jenny raced off to find Vole, Bluejay, and Rabbit. They were happy to share a little bit of the things they had found that morning, and soon Jenny's arms were full as she ran back to her brothers and sister. They squeaked with excitement as Jenny told them her plan.

Soon they were all busy, shredding and sticking, until
at last the present was ready. The little mice ran home.

"Wake up, Mom! Happy birthday!" they giggled. "We've got a present just for you!"

Mother Mouse looked at the picture her children had made. It was red with strawberry, blue with feathers, and sprinkled golden with flower pollen.

"It's beautiful," she smiled, and hugged her mice close. "Thank you, everyone. It's the best birthday present ever."